Everyone is Entitled to
My Opinion

This book was originally published in 2013.
Revised and Re-Published October 2022.
Copyright 2013/2022   Peggy E. Browning
Art designed by Peggy Browning Copyright 2013/2022
All rights reserved
Paperback ISBN: 978-1-954343-14-6
Published by 8th Street Press

For my Children & Grandchildren.
Yes, your Grandma is silly. Thanks for loving me anyway.

"Be silly. Be honest. Be kind." Ralph Waldo Emerson

I've learned a lot through the years…mostly that I shouldn't take myself too seriously. I'm sharing with you some of my life lessons and the life lessons I've gleaned from others. Take a break, drink some wine or a cup of coffee, read this silly book, and laugh a little, then take a nap…you'll feel better soon.

Peggy Browning
…Square Peg

Everyone is Entitled to My Opinion

Peggy Browning

"The best things in life are silly."
--Scott Adams

8TH STREET PRESS
BOOKS BY PEGGY BROWNING & FRIENDS

8thstreetpress@gmail.com
8thstreetpress.com
(940) 538-9645

Be wise, but don't be a wise guy. Laugh at yourself ...go ahead...lighten up. Have fun while you're here because none of us are getting out of here alive.

...Square Peg

Square Peg 2013

It's a miracle that curiosity survives formal education.

http://fifiyodd.com

9

Square Peg 2013

You're never too old
to dream.
You're never too old
to set another goal.
Go for it!

http://fiftyodd.com

Square Peg 2013

Life is a shipwreck
but we must not
forget to sing
in the lifeboats.

http://fiftyodd.com

Square Peg 2013

A positive attitude
may not solve
all your problems,
but it will annoy
enough people to make
it worth your effort.

http://fiftyodd.com

Square Peg 2013

I seldom end up
where I wanted to go,
but almost always
end up
where I need to be.

http://fiftyodd.com

13

Square Peg 2013

Middle Age
is not different
from earlier life
as long as
you're sitting down.

http://fiftyodd.com

Square Peg 2013

Don't talk to me about
Valentine's Day.
At my age
an affair of the heart
is a bypass.

http://fiftyodd.com

15

Square Peg 2013

Old age
is no place
for sissies.

http://fiftyodd.com

Square Peg 2013

Middle age is when
you're sitting at home
on a Saturday night
and the telephone rings
and you hope
it isn't for you.

http://fiftyodd.com

17

Square Peg 2013

The best part of life is
when your family
becomes your friends,
and your friends
become your family.

http://fiftyodd.com

Square Peg 2013

In three words
I can sum up
everything
I've learned about
Life.
It goes on.

http://fijiyodd.com

Square Peg 2013

Every man
is a damn fool for at least
five minutes every day;
wisdom consists in
not exceeding the limit.

http://fiftyodd.com

20

Square Peg 2013

Laugh often.
Dream big.
Reach for the stars.

http://fifiyodd.com

When dealing with people, remember you are not dealing with creatures of logic, but with creatures of emotion, creatures bristling with prejudice, and motivated by pride and vanity.

http://fiftyodd.com

Square Peg 2013

22

The only reason a great
many American families
don't own an elephant
is that they have never been
offered an elephant for a
dollar down and easy
weekly payments.

http://fiftyodd.com

Square Peg 2013

Square Peg 2013

You can never
get enough of
what you don't need
to make you happy.

http://fiftyodd.com

24

Square Peg 2013

In this life we have to take chances. Sometimes they are worth it and sometimes they aren't. But I'm telling you now you will never know until you try.

http://fiftyodd.com

Square Peg 2013

Never take a shortcut
in life, take the long
route because you pick
up more experiences
on the way.

http://fiftyodd.com

26

Square Peg 2013

I'm strong because
I've been weak.
I'm fearless because
I've been afraid.
I'm wise because
I've been foolish.

http://fiftyodd.com

Square Peg 2013

A FRIEND is someone who understands your past, believes in your future, and accepts you just the way you are.

http://fiftyodd.com

Square Peg 2013

Truly great friends are
hard to find,
difficult to leave, and
impossible to forget.

http://fiftyodd.com

29

Square Peg 2013

To become
old and wise…
you have to first be
young and stupid.

http://fiftyodd.com

Square Peg 2013

If you can read this,
thank a teacher.
(I'm serious.)

http://fiftyodd.com

31

Square Peg 2013

None of us got where we are solely by pulling ourselves up by our bootstraps. We got here because somebody ... bent down and helped us pick up our boots.

http://fiftyodd.com

32

Square Peg 2013

Aging is not lost youth
but a new stage of
opportunity and strength.

http://fiftyodd.com

Square Peg 2013

If a window of
opportunity appears,
don't
pull down the shade.

http://fiftyodd.com

34

Square Peg 2013

Don't get too comfortable
with who you are
at any given time -
you may miss the
opportunity to become
who you want to be.

http://fiftyodd.com

35

Square Peg 2013

Don't brood.
Get on with living and loving.
You don't have forever.

http://fiftyodd.com

36

Square Peg 2013

Change
is inevitable…
except from
a vending machine.

http://fiftyodd.com

37

Square Peg 2013

Think something is
impossible to do?
Ask an old broad to do it.
And she *will* get it done.

http://fiftyodd.com

38

Square Peg 2013

Always borrow money
from a pessimist…
they never expect
to get it back.

http://fiftyodd.com

39

Square Peg 2013

Never go on trips
with anyone
you don't love.

http://fiftyodd.com

Square Peg 2013

Two things are infinite:
the universe and
human stupidity;
and I'm not sure
about the universe.

http://fiftyodd.com

Square Peg 2013

One of the advantages
of living on Earth
is that you get
a free annual trip
around the Sun.

http://fiftyodd.com

Square Peg 2013

Those people who tell me that I'm going to hell while they're going to heaven somehow make me very glad that we're going to separate destinations.

http://fiftyodd.com

43

Square Peg 2013

Some people
are born on third base
and go through life
thinking they hit
a triple.

http://fiftyodd.com

Square Peg 2013

Prejudice is a great
time saver.
You can form opinions
without having
to get the facts.

http://fiftyodd.com

Square Peg 2013

We never really
grow up,
we only learn
how to act in public.

http://fiftyodd.com

Square Peg 2013

The early bird might
get the worm,
but the second mouse
gets the cheese.

http://fiftyodd.com

Square Peg 2013

To steal ideas from
one person
is plagiarism.
To steal from many
is research.

http://fiftyodd.com

Square Peg 2013

If God is watching us,
the least we can do
is be entertaining.

http://fijiyodd.com

49

Square Peg 2013

Better to remain silent
and be thought a fool,
than to speak
and remove all doubt.

http://fiftyodd.com

Square Peg 2013

Did you know that dolphins
are so smart that within a few
weeks of captivity,
they can train people to stand
on the very edge of the pool
and throw them fish?

http://fiftyodd.com

51

Square Peg 2013

I thought
I wanted a career,
turns out
I just wanted paychecks.

http://fiftyodd.com

Square Peg 2013

I didn't say
it was your fault,
I *said*
I was blaming you.

http://fijiyodd.com

Square Peg 2013

The shinbone
is a body part
designed especially
for finding furniture
in a dark room.

http://fiftyodd.com

Square Peg 2013

Why
does someone believe you
when you say there are
four billion stars,
but check when you say
the paint is wet?

http://fiftyodd.com

55

Square Peg 2013

Women will never
be equal to men
until they
can walk down the street
with a bald head
and a beer gut,
and still think they are sexy.

http://fiftyodd.com

56

Square Peg 2013

Behind every successful
man is his woman.
Behind the fall
of a successful man is
usually another woman.

http://fijiyodd.com

Square Peg 2013

You don't need
a parachute to skydive.
You only need
a parachute
to skydive *twice*.

http://fiftyodd.com

Square Peg 2013

A clear conscience
is usually
the sign
of a bad memory.

http://fijiyodd.com

Square Peg 2013

Laugh
at your problems,
everybody else does.

http://fiftyodd.com

Square Peg 2013

A diplomat is someone
who can tell you to
go to hell
in such a way that
you will look forward
to the trip.

http://fiftyodd.com

Square Peg 2013

Money
can't buy happiness,
but it sure makes
misery easier
to live with.

http://fiftyodd.com

Square Peg 2013

Worrying works!
90% of the things
I worry about
never happen.

http://fiftyodd.com

Square Peg 2013

Some cause happiness
wherever they go.
Others cause it
whenever they go.

http://fiftyodd.com

Square Peg 2013

I like work.
It fascinates me.
I sit and look at it
for hours.

http://fijiyodd.com

65

Square Peg 2013

You're *never*
too old
to learn
something stupid.

http://fiftyodd.com

Square Peg 2013

When tempted to
fight fire with fire,
remember that
the Fire Department
usually uses water.

http://fiftyodd.com

Square Peg 2013

A bargain
is something
you don't need
at a price
you can't resist.

http://fiftyodd.com

Square Peg 2013

Some people hear voices..
Some see invisible people..
Others have
no imagination
whatsoever.

http://fiftyodd.com

Square Peg 2013

Nostalgia
isn't what it used to be.

http: fiftyodd.com

70

Square Peg 2013

What's the difference between
a northern fairytale and a
southern fairytale?
A northern fairytale begins
"Once upon a time..."
A southern fairytale begins
"Y'all ain't
gonna believe this shit..."

http://fiftyodd.com

71

Square Peg 2013

Haikus are easy.
But sometimes they
don't make sense.
Refrigerator.

http://fiftyodd.com

Square Peg 2013

When you go into court, you are putting your fate into the hands of people who weren't smart enough to get out of jury duty.

http://fiftyodd.com

73

Square Peg 2013

Children seldom
misquote you.
In fact, they usually
repeat word for word
what you shouldn't
have said.

http://fiftyodd.com

Square Peg 2013

Some mistakes
are too much fun
to only make once.

http://fiftyodd.com

Square Peg 2013

Deja Vu -
When you think you're
doing something you've
done before,
it's because God thought
it was so funny, he had to
rewind it for his friends.

http://fiftyodd.com

Square Peg 2013

If you can stay calm
while all around you
is chaos, then you
probably haven't
completely understood
the situation.

http://fiftyodd.com

Square Peg 2013

If you can't
convince them,
confuse them.

http://fiftyodd.com

Square Peg 2013

If you always keep
your feet firmly
on the ground,
you'll have trouble
putting on your pants.

http://fiftyodd.com

Square Peg 2013

Americans will sail
across an ocean
to fight a war,
but won't bother to
cross the street to vote.

http://fiftyodd.com

Square Peg 2013

To err is human,
to blame it
on somebody else
shows
management potential.

http://fiftyodd.com

Square Peg 2013

We are all
time travelers
moving at the speed
of exactly
60 minutes per hour.

http://fiftyodd.com

82

Square Peg 2013

Experience
is what you get
when you didn't get
what you wanted.

http://fiftyodd.com

83

Square Peg 2013

People tend to
make rules for others
and exceptions for
themselves.

http://fiftyodd.com

84

Square Peg 2013

I have all the money
I'll ever need ...
if I die by 4:00 p.m.
today.

http://fiftyodd.com

85

Square Peg 2013

Alcohol
is not the answer,
it just makes you
forget the question.

http://fiftyodd.com

Square Peg 2013

The difference
between fiction
and reality?
Fiction has to make sense.

http://fiftyodd.com

Square Peg 2013

It's so simple to be wise.
Just think of
something stupid to say
and then don't say it.

http://fiftyodd.com

Square Peg 2013

What is the
most important thing
to learn in chemistry?
Never lick the spoon.

http://fiftyodd.com

Square Peg 2013

There are two kinds of friends : those who are around when you need them, and those who are around when *they* need *you*.

http://fiftyodd.com

90

Square Peg 2013

The trouble with doing something right the first time is that nobody appreciates how difficult it was.

http://fiftyodd.com

Square Peg 2013

I have to exercise
early in the morning
before my brain
figures out
what I'm doing.

http://fiftyodd.com

Square Peg 2013

Lite:
the new way to spell
"Light,"
now with 20% fewer letters!

http://fifiyodd.com

93

Square Peg 2013

Efficiency
is a highly developed
form of laziness.

http://fiftyodd.com

94

It's not
how good your work is,
it's how well
you explain it.

http://fiftyodd.com

Square Peg 2013

Some of us learn from
the mistakes of others;
the rest of us
have to be the others.

http://fiftyodd.com

Square Peg 2013

People
will believe anything
if you whisper it.

http://fiftyodd.com

Square Peg 2013

Be careful of
your thoughts,
they may become
WORDS
at any moment.

http://fiftyodd.com

Square Peg 2013

The farther away
the future is,
the better it looks.

http://fijiyodd.com

Square Peg 2013

There are
two kinds of people
who don't say much:
those who are quiet
and those who talk a lot.

http://fiftyodd.com

Square Peg 2013

If
you don't say it,
they can't repeat it.

http://fiftyodd.com

Square Peg 2013

Anyone
who has never made
a mistake
has never tried
anything new.

http://fiftyodd.com

Square Peg 2013

If you don't care
where you are,
then you ain't lost.

http://fifyodd.com

Square Peg 2013

A clean desk
is a sign
of a cluttered desk drawer.

http://fiftyodd.com

104

Square Peg 2013

I just
let my mind wander,
but it didn't
come back yet.

http://fiftyodd.com

Square Peg 2013

Oh Lord,
give me patience,
and
GIVE IT TO ME NOW!

http://fiftyodd.com

Square Peg 2013

I don't believe
in miracles.
I rely on them.

http://fiftyodd.com

Square Peg 2013

A proverb is
a short sentence
based on
long experience.

http://fiftyodd.com

Square Peg 2013

I don't
necessarily agree
with everything I say.

http://fiftyodd.com

Square Peg 2013

One nice thing
about egotists:
They don't talk about
other people.

http://fiftyodd.com

Square Peg 2013

Do you know the difference between education and experience? Education is when you read the fine print; experience is what you get when you don't.

http://fiftyodd.com

111

Square Peg 2013

Everything has been
said before, but since
nobody listens
we have to keep going
back and beginning
all over again.

http://fiftyodd.com

112

Square Peg 2013

If we could sell
our experiences for what
they cost us,
we'd all be millionaires.

http://fiftyodd.com

Square Peg 2013

There must
be more to life
than having
everything!

http://fiftyodd.com

114

Everyone has flaws.
Even the best of us
has a crack in her butt.

http://fiftyodd.com

Square Peg 2013

Square Peg 2013

And…
this is just one
more day that
I didn't use algebra!

http://fiftyodd.com

THE END

I learn from experience…boy, do I! …and I also learn from the wisdom passed to me by others. (Although I have a short attention span, I am a bad listener, and I learn best from making my own mistakes.) Some things are so interesting that I have to experience them again and again before I fully understand them.

I have taken the best of quotes from persons known and unknown and had Square Peg share them with you.

The quotes used here are listed by "quoter" and by page number. *The following quotes are attributed to:*

P. 9	*Albert Einstein*
P. 10	*Square Peg (hereafter known as SP)*

Thank you for reading my silliness.
I appreciate your readership.
Have a great day.

And...be sure to check out my website at
8thstreetpress.com

15058431R00071